Winnie-the-Pooh

Winnie-the-Pooh
Tiggers Don't Climb Trees

Based on the stories by A. A. Milne

One day, when Pooh was sitting on a stone in the middle of the stream, thinking, he thought he would go and see Eeyore. He walked along, singing a little song to himself, when he thought he would go and see Owl instead as he hadn't seen him since the day before yesterday. But then he remembered Kanga, Roo and Tigger. And, of course, there was Rabbit. "I like talking to Rabbit," thought Pooh. Before he knew it, Pooh was back at his own front door again. And it was eleven o'clock. Which was Time-for-a-little-something....

Half an hour later he was doing what he had always really meant to do, he was stumping off to Piglet's house.

Piglet was busy digging a small hole in the ground outside his house.

"Hallo, Piglet," said Pooh. "What are you doing?"

"I'm planting a haycorn, Pooh, so that it can grow up into an oak-tree, and have lots of haycorns just outside the front door instead of having to walk miles and miles, do you see, Pooh?"

"Supposing it doesn't?" said Pooh.

"It will, because Christopher Robin says it will, so that's why I'm planting it."

And he put the acorn in the hole he had made, and covered it up with earth, and jumped on it.

When Piglet had finished jumping, he wiped his paws on his front, and said, "What shall we do now?" and Pooh said, "Let's go and see Kanga and Roo and Tigger." So they set off for Kanga's house.

Now, Kanga had felt rather motherly that morning, and wanted to count things – like Roo's vests, and how many pieces of soap there were left; so she sent them out with a packet of watercress sandwiches for Roo and a packet of extract-of-malt sandwiches for Tigger, to have a nice long morning in the Forest not getting into mischief. And off they had gone.

And as they went, Tigger told Roo all about the things that Tiggers could do.

"Can they fly?" asked Roo.

"Yes," said Tigger, "they're very good flyers, Tiggers are. Strornry good flyers."

"Oo!" said Roo. "Can they fly as well as Owl?"

"Yes," said Tigger. "Only they don't want to."

Roo couldn't understand this, because he thought it would be lovely to be able to fly, but Tigger said it was difficult to explain to anybody who wasn't a Tigger himself.

"Can they jump as far as Kangas?" asked Roo.

"Yes," said Tigger. "When they want to."

In a little while they came to the Six Pine Trees.

"I can swim," said Roo. "Can Tiggers swim?"

"Of course they can. Tiggers can do everything."

"Can they climb trees better than Pooh?" asked Roo, stopping under the tallest Pine Tree, and looking up at it.

"Climbing trees is what they do best," said Tigger. "Much better than Poohs."

"Could they climb this one?"

"I'll show you," said Tigger bravely, "and you can sit on my back and watch me."

"Oo, Tigger!" squeaked Roo excitedly.

So he sat on Tigger's back and up they went.

For the first ten feet Tigger said happily to himself, "Up we go!"

For the next ten feet he said:

"I always *said* Tiggers could climb trees."

And for the next ten feet he said:

"Not that it's easy, mind you."

And for the next ten feet he said:

"Of course, there's the coming down too. Backwards."

And then he said:

"Which will be difficult ..."

"Unless one fell ..."

"When it would be ..."

"EASY."

And at the word "easy", the branch he was standing on broke and he just managed to clutch at the one above him as he felt himself going....

Slowly he scrambled upwards … until at last he was sitting on it, breathing quickly, and wishing that he had gone in for swimming instead.

Roo climbed off, and sat down next to him.

"Tigger," he said excitedly, "are we at the top?"

"No," said Tigger.

"Are we going to the top?"

"*No*," said Tigger.

"Oh!" said Roo rather sadly. Then he went on hopefully: "That was a lovely bit when you pretended we were going to fall-bump-to-the-bottom, and we didn't. Will you do that bit again?"

"NO," said Tigger.

Roo was silent for a little while, and then he said, "Shall we eat our sandwiches, Tigger?" And Tigger said, "Yes, where are they?" And Roo said, "At the bottom of the tree." And Tigger said, "I don't think we'd better eat them just yet." So they didn't.

By-and-by Pooh and Piglet came walking along.

"Look, Pooh!" said Piglet suddenly. "There's something in one of the Pine Trees."

"So there is!" said Pooh, looking up wonderingly. "There's an Animal."

Piglet took Pooh's arm, in case Pooh was frightened.

"Is it One of the Fiercer Animals?" he said, looking the other way.

Pooh nodded.

"It's a Jagular," he said.

"What do Jagulars do?" asked Piglet, hoping that they wouldn't.

"They hide in the branches of trees, and drop on you as you go underneath," said Pooh. "Christopher Robin told me."

Suddenly the Jagular called out to them.

"Help! Help!" it called.

"That's what Jagulars always do," said Pooh knowledgeably.

Something very excited next to the Jagular heard him and squeaked:

"Pooh and Piglet! Pooh and Piglet!"

"Pooh!" Piglet cried. "I believe it's Tigger and Roo!"

"So it is," said Pooh. "I thought it was a Jagular and another Jagular."

"What are you doing?" called Piglet.

"We can't get down, we can't get down!" cried Roo.

"How did you get there, Roo?" asked Piglet.

"On Tigger's back! And Tiggers can't climb downwards, because their tails get in the way, and Tigger forgot about that when we started, and he's only just remembered. So we've got to stay here for ever and ever – unless we go higher. What did you say, Tigger? Oh, Tigger says if we go higher we shan't be able to see Piglet's house so well, so we're going to stop here."

"Piglet," said Pooh solemnly, "I think they're stuck." And he began to eat Tigger's sandwiches.

"Couldn't you climb up to them?"
asked Piglet.

"I might, Piglet, and I might
bring Roo down on my back, but
I couldn't bring Tigger down.
We must think of something else."
In a thoughtful way he began to eat
Roo's sandwiches, as well.

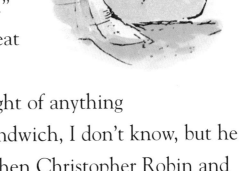

Whether he would have thought of anything
before he had finished the last sandwich, I don't know, but he
had just got to the last but one when Christopher Robin and
Eeyore came strolling along together.

"There's Pooh!" said Christopher Robin. "Hallo, Pooh!"

"It's Christopher Robin!" said Piglet. "*He'll* know what to do."

They hurried up to him.

"Oh, Christopher Robin," began Pooh.

"And Eeyore," said Eeyore.

"Tigger and Roo are up the Six Pine Trees, and they can't get down, and –"

"And I was just saying," put in Piglet, "that if only Christopher Robin –"

"*And* Eeyore –"

"If only you were here, then we could think of something to do."

Christopher Robin looked up at Tigger and Roo, and tried to think of something.

"*I* thought," said Piglet earnestly, "that if Eeyore stood at the bottom of the tree, and if Pooh stood on Eeyore's back, and if I stood on Pooh's shoulders –"

"And if Eeyore's back snapped suddenly, then we could all laugh," said Eeyore.

"Would it break your back, Eeyore?" asked Pooh, surprised.

"That's what would be so interesting – not being quite sure till afterwards."

Pooh said "Oh!" and they all began to think again.

"I've got an idea!" cried Christopher Robin suddenly. "I'll take off my tunic and we'll each hold a corner, and then Roo and Tigger can jump into it. They won't hurt themselves."

When Roo understood what he had to do, he was wildly excited, and cried out: "Tigger, we're going to jump! Tigger! Like flying, my jumping will be. Can Tiggers do it?" And he squeaked out: "I'm coming, Christopher Robin!" and he jumped – straight into the middle of the tunic.

He bounced and bounced – and went on bouncing and saying "Oo!" for quite a long time.

"Come on, Tigger," he called out. "It's easy."

But Tigger was holding on to the branch.

"Just wait a moment," said Tigger nervously. "Small piece of bark in my eye." And he moved slowly along his branch.

And suddenly Tigger found how easy it was.

"Ow!" he shouted as the tree flew past him.

"Look out!" cried Christopher Robin to the others.

There was a crash, and a tearing noise, and a confused heap of everybody on the ground.

Underneath everybody else was Eeyore.

"Oh, Eeyore!" cried Christopher Robin. "Are you hurt?"

Eeyore said nothing for a long time. And then he said:
"Is Tigger there?"

Tigger was there, feeling Bouncy again already.

"Yes," said Christopher Robin. "Tigger's here."

"Well, just thank him for me," said Eeyore.